This edition published by Parragon in 2010

Parragon
Queen Street House
4 Queen Street
Bath BA1 1HE, Bath, UK

Copyright © Parragon Books Ltd 2006

ISBN 978-1-4054-7605-8
Printed in China

Polar Bear and the Rainbow

Illustrated by Sanja Rescek   Written by Moira Butterfield

PaRRagon

Bath · New York · Singapore · Hong Kong · Cologne · Delhi · Melbourne

Ben, the little polar bear, was the same color as snow.
He was the same color as his sister and his mom.
He was the same color as polar bears everywhere.

"How b-o-r-i-n-g," thought Ben.

Ben watched the sunrise with his friends the hare and the fox. "You look pink in the new sunlight," they told him.

"I'm pink! I'm pink!" cried Ben. But as the sun climbed higher, he turned back to the color of snow.

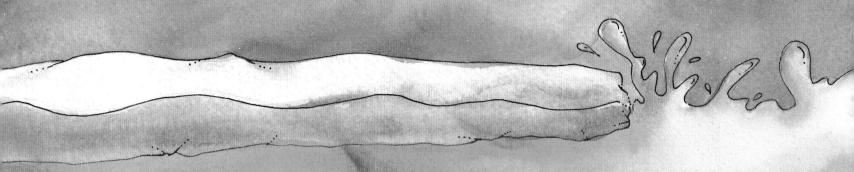

Ben went swimming with his friend the seal.
"You look blue in the water," she told him.

"I'm blue! I'm blue!" cried Ben. But when he climbed out of the water, he turned back to the color of his sister and his mom.

That night, Ben dreamed that he was
as bright and sparkly as a rainbow.

Poor Ben. When he woke up his
rainbow fur had disappeared.

The next day, Ben found a snowman. He had a big smile made of stones.

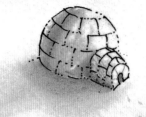

"The snowman is the same color as me, and he looks very happy," thought Ben.

Then Ben played hide-and-seek with his friends.

"Where are you, Ben?"

"We give up, Ben."

"You win, Ben. We can't see you."

"The snow is the same color as me.
That's why I'm good at hide-and-seek," thought Ben.

Soon sparkly white snowflakes began to fall all around. The snowflakes felt tingly on Ben's nose.

"Snowflakes are the same color as me, and they are beautiful," thought Ben.

At the end of the day, Ben cuddled up with
his family.

"I don't think I mind being polar bear-colored
after all. I am the same color as smiley snowmen
and sparkly snowflakes," he thought.

Best of all, he was the same color as his sister and his mom. They were soft and snuggly, like polar bears everywhere, and he loved them very much.